This book is dedicated to everyone who has ever laughed at their own trumps!

Also, special thanks to my sister, Lynn, for the hours spent co-editing, travelling by train between London and Liverpool. And thanks to Kate for all the finishing touches.

LITTLE TIGER PRESS
An imprint of Magi Publications
1 The Coda Centre, 189 Munster Road, London SW6 6AW
www.littletigerpress.com

First published in Great Britain 2004
This edition published 2008

A CIP catalogue record for this book is available
from the British Library
All rights reserved • ISBN 978-1-84506-704-5

Printed in China

2 4 6 8 10 9 7 5 3 1

POOH!
IS THAT YOU, BERTIE?

David Roberts

LITTLE TIGER PRESS
London

This is Bertie.
He likes making smells.

POOT

At the dentist Bertie let off a little poot.
It ponged.

"POOH!

IS THAT YOU, BERTIE?

That's not polite,"
sniffed Mum.

Bertie let off a big parp in the art gallery and giggled. No one else did. It ponged.

"POOH!
IS THAT YOU, BERTIE?

I've never been so embarrassed,"
sniffed Dad.

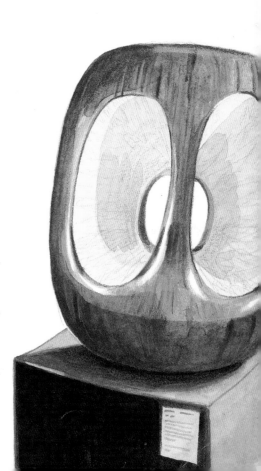

At the café Bertie let off a smelly boff.
It ponged worse than a bad egg.

"POOH!

IS THAT YOU, BERTIE?

It's not nice to break wind in the café,
not when people are eating,"
sniffed Gran.

Bertie let rip a tremendous trump in big sister Suzy's playhouse. It ponged. Suzy was livid.

"POOH!

IS THAT YOU, BERTIE?

You stink, smelly pants,"
sniffed Suzy.

It's not fair! thought Bertie.
I'm not the only one who stinks.

When Mum lets off a poot, she coughs
at the same time to cover it up.

When Dad lets off he's so sneaky . . .

you don't know what's coming
until it hits you.

Gran's always letting rip.
She just blames the cat.

Suzy claims she never trumps.
But she sounds like a brass band
when she thinks no one's listening!

PRRRRP

FRRRP

PARP

And when the dog boffs,
he wafts it about!

So there, everybody does it!

But _I_ do it best . . .

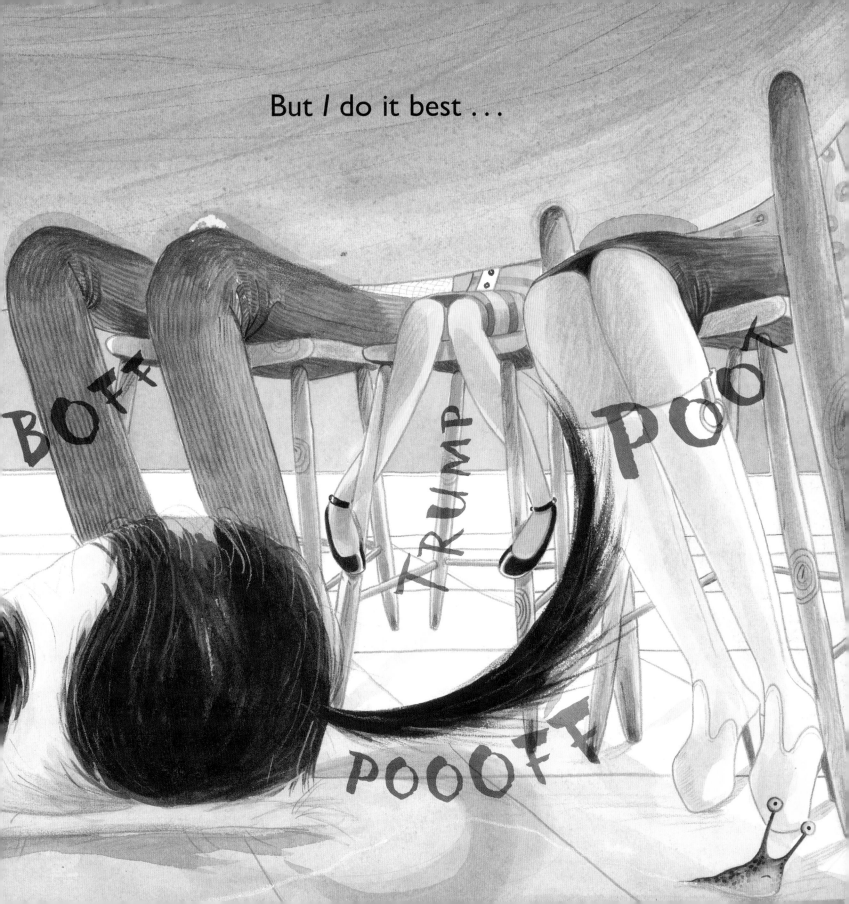

Especially in the bath!

Sing along with Dirty Bertie!

First Verse

Chorus

Other recent titles in this series

For information regarding any other
Little Tiger Tales Picture Book and CD Sets,
or for our catalogue, please contact us:
Little Tiger Press, 1 The Coda Centre,
189 Munster Road, London SW6 6AW, UK
Tel: 020 7385 6333 Fax: 020 7385 7333
e-mail: info@littletiger.co.uk
www.littletigerpress.com

Oh, Bertie was a trumper;
He loved to make a smell.
He farted at the dentist's
And made his mother yell . . .

Chorus:
Pooh, Bertie, Pooh!
Bertie, is that you?
Oh, please don't make us sniff
Your most unpleasant whiff!

Bertie went to see
Some fascinating art.
His dad was not impressed
With Bertie's massive fart!

Chorus

Bertie's granny was sniffy
when Bertie was whiffy;
"It's not nice," she would beg.
"And it pongs of bad egg."
She would hold her nose,
splutter and cough
When Bertie at the table let off a boff!

Chorus

And when Bertie did a trump
While he sipped a cup of tea
His poor sister got the hump
And said, "Get away from me!
You're a dirty boy, that's what I think,
With smelly pants – you really stink!"

Chorus

Not fair! thinks Bertie,
When I'm not the one
Who poots in the kitchen
And coughs as it's done.
Not me who lies on the couch
And then lifts a
Leg to let out a great big,
Eggy drifter!

Although I confess,
I am probably best
At the worst kind of fart crime . . .
Making bubbles at bath time!

Chorus x 2